JANE EYRE

CHARLOTTE BRONTË

w⋯ ⋯.co.uk

Retold by Gill Tavner
Illustrated by Vanessa Lubach

Published by Real Reads Ltd
Stroud, Gloucestershire, UK
www.realreads.co.uk

First published in 2009
Reprinted 2011

ISBN 978-1-906230-21-0

Printed in China by Wai Man Book Binding (China) Ltd
Designed by Lucy Guenot
Typeset by Bookcraft Ltd, Stroud, Gloucestershire

CONTENTS

THE CHARACTERS

Jane Eyre

Plain, small, and orphaned, Jane is alone in the world. Will she ever find the adventure she seeks and the affection she so desperately needs?

Mrs Reed

Mrs Reed is Jane's cold, cruel aunt. Does she have the power to make Jane miserable for ever?

Helen Burns

Gentle Helen is Jane's best friend. How will she influence Jane? Is she strong enough to survive?

Mr Rochester

Mr Rochester is dark and brooding, but full of fire. Why does he hate his home? What secret does he keep locked away?

Adèle

Adèle is Mr Rochester's charge and Jane's pupil. Will she like her new governess?

Grace Poole

Why does this servant live alone on the third storey? Is it she who haunts the night with savage laughter? What is her deadly secret?

St John Rivers

St John (pronounced 'Sinjun') is handsome and clever. Will he help to heal Jane's broken heart?

JANE EYRE

'Where are you Jane, you ugly rat? Come out, wherever you are.'

I cowered, cross-legged on the window seat behind the crimson curtain, my book still open in my trembling lap.

My cousin John flung back the curtain. 'There you are! Stand up immediately!'

I obeyed him. 'What do you want?'

'Say, "What do you want, Master Reed?"'

I forced myself to raise my eyes to his face. 'What do you want, Master Reed?'

Four years older than me, with dull eyes and overfed cheeks, John Reed bullied me continuously. Every part of my ten-year-old body feared him. Now, I waited for him to hit me. He struck me hard. I tottered backwards, hitting my head against the door frame. My head bled. 'Stand up, orphan,' shouted John. 'You should be begging in the streets, not living here at mama's expense.'

The fire of rebellion ignited within me. 'You are wicked and cruel,' I shouted.

John ran headlong at me, calling, 'Mama, help me! Jane is in a fury!' We struggled together for a few minutes before my aunt appeared with Bessie, her servant.

'Take her to the red room, and lock her in,' Mrs Reed commanded.

Once the fire in my blood had cooled, I looked around me. My prison was a large, stately room which had been left cold and silent since my uncle died in there nine years ago.

My parents had died of typhus when I was a baby. My uncle had vowed to take care of me, but his own untimely death one year later left this responsibility to his resentful wife. What would he have thought of my imprisonment?

The hours passed. I grew as cold as stone. The eerie light of the autumn evening stirred my imagination. What if my uncle's ghost appeared now, in this room in which he had died? My heart beat rapidly. My head grew hot. Fear possessed me, and I threw myself against the door. 'Let me out! Let me out!'

My aunt's angry footsteps stopped outside. 'For this outburst,' her cold voice decreed, 'you must stay an extra hour.'

'Oh aunt, have pity,' I sobbed.

She walked away.

Autumn became winter. One cold January morning, summoned to my aunt's presence, I found myself standing before a tall man dressed in black.

'I'm sending you to boarding school,' my aunt told me. 'This is Mr Brocklehurst, the master of the school.'

The man looked down at me with stony eyes. 'You are small and plain,' he observed. 'Are you a good little girl?'

His deep voice scared me. I was unable to answer.

My aunt filled the silence. 'I am afraid she has many faults, Mr Brocklehurst, the worst of which is deceit. Warn her teachers.'

'Deceit!' boomed Mr Brocklehurst. He stooped to look into my eyes. 'Deceitful children go to hell.' He turned back to my aunt. 'I shall warn everybody.'

I struggled to suppress a sob. I now fully understood my aunt's power to wound me. However hard I tried, I had never won her affection. Now, she sowed her hatred and unkindness along my future path.

'Keep her humble, Mr Brocklehurst. I never want to see her again.'

On the day of my departure, I burned with resentment for the treatment I had received from my aunt in the past, and the treatment she had ensured me in the future. As I stood before her to say farewell, her icy eyes dwelt freezingly upon me, but they failed to cool my fire. Something over which I had no control spoke out of me. 'I will never call you aunt again,' I trembled. 'Your miserable cruelty makes me sick. *You* are deceitful, not I. You think, because I am poor and plain, that I can live without any human kindness. I cannot.'

My aunt stood, cold and silent as an iceberg. Bessie gently guided me into the awaiting coach. I was to travel to Lowood alone.

Lowood School sat in a dark, damp dell. Entering the grounds, I saw girls huddling in groups, with no shelter from the wind and rain. They were all without proper boots or gloves, their brown dresses offering insufficient protection. All were pale and thin.

On my first morning, in the cold, dimly-lit dining room, I learned that the food at Lowood was tasteless and inadequate. From that moment, my stomach ached for food. As I passed the teachers' table on my way out, I heard an elegant lady dressed in purple whisper, 'What abominable food! How shameful!'

As the weeks passed, we were all weakened by cold and hunger. We gathered ever closer around the small fires. Although usually absent, Mr Brocklehurst kept strict control over Lowood's budget, allowing very little for food, clothing or fuel. Occasionally, the elegant teacher in purple would secure for us a little extra bread. 'Miss Temple is the kindest teacher,' my new friend Helen Burns told me. 'She is full of goodness.'

I made good progress in my studies and the other girls accepted me. With Helen Burns' friendship I was, in my own way, happy. I had just one fear. When would Mr Brocklehurst appear and turn everybody against me?

The dreaded day arrived. Like a tower of cold black marble, Mr Brocklehurst stood before us. 'You!' he shouted, pointing to one of the older girls whose curly red hair was rebelling against her morning's attempts to tie it neatly. 'Your hair must be cut off entirely. Such vanity is not acceptable. You must learn modesty and duty.'

Then he looked at me. I saw recognition in his eyes. 'Little girl!' he boomed. 'Come here.' He pulled a stool towards me. 'Stand upon this stool.'

Trembling, I did as I was bid.

'Teachers and children,' he addressed our audience. 'The devil has found a servant in this girl. Exclude her from your games. Do not talk to her. This girl,' he announced, 'is a liar!'

There was silence. I felt everybody's eyes burning into me.

Mr Brocklehurst tied a label saying 'Liar' around my neck. 'Let her stand half an hour upon this stool.'

Hot tears of anger and humiliation threatened to escape from my eyes. Hearing a cough, I looked up to see Helen, her eyes shining with kindness. She smiled gently at me: a smile of true understanding and courage. My tears subsided. Around Helen's neck I saw the familiar 'Untidy' label she was often forced to wear.

Poor Helen was frequently punished by one cruel teacher for her untidy ways. She bore the cane's sting patiently. 'My punishments are deserved, so it is easy to bear them,' she once told me. 'It is true, I *am* careless and untidy.'

'But I would seize the cane and break it,' I had replied.

'Life is too short for disagreements,' coughed Helen. 'We should love our enemies.'

Now, standing on the stool, I bore my punishment because I had to. I could not copy Helen's calm acceptance.

That evening, Miss Temple invited Helen and me to her room. I held my head low. What must she think of me now?

'Jane,' Miss Temple soothed, 'we shall think of you as we know you to be. Can you explain why Mr Brocklehurst accused you of deceit?'

Choking with tears, I told Miss Temple and Helen all about my aunt. Miss Temple smiled. 'Your name is now clear. I will ensure that everybody knows.'

'You should try to forgive.' Helen breathed with difficulty, and I noticed that her hollow cough was becoming more frequent. 'Do not bear resentment when life is so short. Our reward is in heaven.'

Miss Temple looked sadly at Helen's pale face. When we stood to leave, she gave us each a gentle hug. I noticed that she gave a low sigh when she held Helen.

Spring came, but the welcome sunshine was too gentle to combat the damp of Lowood's situation.

Disease took a deadly hold of Lowood. Many girls died. Others escaped to relatives' homes. Lessons were suspended, and any girls free of illness were able to roam in the woods.

I was still young. Enjoying my new freedom, I failed to realise how ill Helen had become. One evening, unable to sleep, I crept into Miss Temple's room, where Helen was being nursed.

'How sad to be lying on a sickbed when the world is so pleasant!' I exclaimed.

Helen smiled weakly. 'You are just in time to bid me goodbye,' she whispered.

'Are you going home?' I was puzzled.

A coughing fit seized Helen. When it had passed, she lay back, exhausted. 'No Jane, I am going to god.'

I was silent. Tears filled my eyes.

'I am happy, Jane. I look forward to heaven.'

'Might I sleep beside you?' I whispered. I put my arms around my friend's neck, and rested my cheek against hers.

'Your warmth is comforting,' sighed Helen. 'Good night Jane.'

'Good night Helen.'

Miss Temple found me asleep the next morning, still holding my dear, dead friend.

Following the deaths of so many girls, Mr Brocklehurst was replaced by a committee of men who built a new school in a healthier situation. I stayed eight years at Lowood in total: six as a student and two as a teacher. I was happy there.

At the age of eighteen, however, I longed for more. I frequently gazed at the distant horizon, and a desire grew within me to follow the road further than I could see. A world full of hopes, fears, excitement and knowledge beckoned to me. I yearned for liberty.

I decided to advertise my services as a governess.

My advertisement attracted only one response, but that was all I needed. A few days later, I left the familiarity of Lowood for an unknown future as governess at Thornfield Hall. The journey was long. Although I felt the thrill of adventure and pride in my independence, I also felt the steady throb of fear.

I needn't have been afraid. I received a warm welcome at Thornfield. The housekeeper, Mrs Fairfax, maintained an atmosphere of domestic comfort. I met my new pupil, Adèle, a lively

eight-year-old French girl, who was delighted by the French I had learned at Lowood. We soon grew fond of each other.

Adèle, accustomed to the finery of French fashion, often commented that my appearance was plain. I sometimes wished to be beautiful, to have rosy cheeks, a straight nose and a tall, stately figure. Instead, I was small and pale, with irregular features.

One evening, I asked Mrs Fairfax about our absent master.

'Mr Rochester is a good man,' she told me, 'although a little peculiar. I'm never sure whether he's serious or joking when he talks to me.'

'Is he often at Thornfield?'

'Very rarely, and we never know when to expect him.'

I wondered why a man would choose to be absent from such a comfortable home. I wondered what Mr Rochester was like.

Despite my developing happiness, restlessness was, and still is, in my nature. I always wonder what lies beyond the horizon. It seems most unfair that men are free to travel, to learn and experience life whilst women are expected to be contented with baking, knitting and embroidering.

Mrs Fairfax satisfied a little of my curiosity by showing me around Thornfield. Its size and style earned my admiration. The third storey, however, which was above my own room, was darker and

gloomier than the rest. 'If there were a ghost at Thornfield,' I mused, 'this is where it would haunt.'

As we walked softly along the darkest passage, between the closed doors of empty rooms, an unexpected sound startled me. A strange laugh, hollow, low and joyless, echoed around us. It was a tragic, unnatural sound.

'Grace!' called Mrs Fairfax. 'Too much noise!'

A solid woman with a hard face appeared from a door. She apologised to Mrs Fairfax and returned to the room.

'Grace Poole does the sewing,' was Mrs Fairfax's unsatisfactory explanation.

I loved venturing beyond Thornfield. One cold afternoon I set out to deliver a letter. An early moon shone eerily through the freezing mist in the silent lanes. Enjoying the stillness, I was suddenly unnerved by the featureless, spectral silhouette of a man on horseback.

As he passed, his horse slipped on some ice. The horse and its mortal rider crashed to the ground.

'Are you injured, sir? Can I help?'

'Stand aside,' the man panted, freeing himself from his horse and pulling it, stamping and clattering, to its feet. 'I only have a sprain,' he grimaced.

His rough, frowning manner gave me more confidence than politeness would have done. 'I will not leave you, sir, until I see that you can mount your horse.'

'Then support me a moment,' he said, leaning his tall body

against me. 'You should be at home yourself by now,' he observed. 'Where are you from?'

'From Thornfield, sir. I am the new governess.'

'Ah! The governess! I had forgotten!' He mounted his horse with some pain. 'Hurry home. It will soon be dark.'

Once I had posted the letter, I returned reluctantly to the confines of Thornfield, where a surprise awaited me. Mrs Fairfax greeted me at the door. 'The master is here,' she bustled. 'He is injured. His horse slipped on some ice.'

'Ah, the roadside elf,' a voice called from the dining room. 'Come in here and greet me.'

I found Mr Rochester alone before the fire, his bandaged foot raised before him.

'So, you are the supernatural being who bewitched my horse. I have you to thank for this injury.'

I stepped forward. He was not an attractive

man, but I saw intelligence in his dark features, and humour sparkled in his eyes. He invited me to sit down. 'Mrs Fairfax tells me that you have taken great pains with Adèle and that she has made much improvement. Thank you.'

I nodded and remained silent.

'Do you play the piano?' he asked.

'A little.'

'Play me a tune,' he ordered. He must have seen the resistance in my eyes, for he checked himself. 'Excuse my tone of command, Miss Eyre. It is habit. Would you please play me a tune?'

I did as I was bid.

'Hmm, you play better than many, but not well.'

Mrs Fairfax met me on the stairs that night as I retired to my room. 'You must excuse the master's manner,' she whispered. 'He has painful thoughts. He leads an unsettled life and dislikes being at Thornfield.'

Mr Rochester's presence brought new life to Thornfield. On many occasions, he invited me to talk with him. I think he feared solitude.

'Do you think me handsome, Miss Eyre?' he asked one evening.

'No, sir.'

'By my word!' he exclaimed in surprise. 'You seem so timid, yet you speak so bluntly. What fault do you find in me? Answer honestly.'

I apologised for my words, but I could not disown them.

'Can you see any signs of the good man that I should have been had not fate decreed otherwise?' He sat thoughtfully for a while.

I watched him.

'How your eyes search my face and character, Miss Eyre. What do you see? Speak.'

I remained silent.

'Ah. I asked rudely again. I apologise, but cannot I claim superiority over you in both age and experience, having roamed over half of the world?'

'That depends very much upon the use
you have made of your years and experience,'
I answered.

One afternoon, as we walked in the garden,
Mr Rochester seemed troubled. 'I envy your clear
conscience, Miss Eyre. I am poisoned by remorse.
I am burdened, cursed by my past.' He looked
up towards the third storey of his home, his eyes
burning with sudden anger. He looked down at me
and sighed. 'Miss Eyre, I find you refresh me.'

My master was no longer unattractive to me:
his face made me happy, his presence cheered me.

The night after our garden walk, my sleep was disturbed by a strange sound outside my chamber door. I sat bolt upright, chilled with fear. It was the same low, eerie laughter I had heard in the dark corridor.

'Who is there?' I called.

The laughter stopped. Silence. I could scarcely breathe.

A moaning, gurgling sound replaced the laughter. It moved away from my door. Why did Grace Poole laugh such an evil laugh? What was she doing now? I could smell smoke, so I rose to investigate. Peering from my room into the darkness, I saw thick smoke billowing from Mr Rochester's door.

In an instant, I was in his room. Tongues of flame licked the bed, in the middle of which my master lay motionless, asleep.

'Wake! Wake!' I cried. I rushed to his basin, seized his water jug and deluged the bed and its occupant. I then flew to my room for more water, which I threw again upon the sleeper. This time

I succeeded in extinguishing the fire and waking
Mr Rochester.

'Good god, Miss Eyre, you wicked elf!' he
cried. 'Are you trying to drown me?'

When Mr Rochester heard my explanation,
the blood left his cheeks. 'I must go upstairs.
Return to bed, Miss Eyre.'

I tried to leave, but his hand still held my
shoulder. 'Jane, you saved me from a horrible
death.' His lips trembled. 'Thank you, my
cherished preserver.'

'You are just a poor, plain governess,' I chastised myself. 'He is too far above you in status and wealth. Do not be so foolish as to imagine yourself his favourite, it can only lead to heartbreak.'

Over the following weeks, I had further reason for caution. Mr Rochester invited to Thornfield a party of friends of such high-born elegance as I had never seen before. Amongst them was the beautiful Blanche Ingram. I watched the group with interest, and it soon became evident that she considered herself Mr Rochester's favourite.

Some evenings, I took a seat in the corner of the room, watching the assembled party. Although I was often in his presence, I felt excluded from Mr Rochester's company. I felt this most severely when he and Miss Ingram moved towards the piano to sing a duet.

In spite of my efforts, I loved Mr Rochester. Although rank and wealth would always divide us, something in my brain, heart and blood joined us together. 'Whilst I breathe and think,' I realised with a shock, 'I must love him.'

At the piano, Mr Rochester and Miss Ingram's voices blended beautifully. Unable to bear it, I left the room and stood outside the door, trying to compose myself. Seconds later, Mr Rochester was beside me.

'Jane, you are pale.' He looked at me with tender concern. 'Are you alright?'

I protested that I was tired and must be allowed to retire to bed.

He nodded. 'Goodnight, my ... ' He stopped and bit his lip.

Though I watched closely, I saw no such tenderness in his eyes when he looked at Miss Ingram. If he married her, it would be for family and for rank, but not for love. I grieved for him.

The following evening, Thornfield received another guest. When I announced Mr Mason's arrival, Mr Rochester grew pale. 'When will there be an end to all this?' he sighed. However, he soon seemed master both of himself and his new guest.

That night, my sleep was once again disturbed. Once again, I sat bolt upright in bed, my heart racing. Above me, on the third storey, I heard bangs and loud stamping noises. A man's voice cried 'Help! Rochester! For god's sake, help!'

Horror shook my limbs as I heard Mr Rochester run from his room. A loud crash. Silence.

Minutes later, I was dressed. Mr Rochester arrived at my door, his eyes darting sparks. 'Jane, do you mind the sight of blood?'

'No sir.'

'Then bring water and a sponge.'

Fearfully, I followed him upstairs to a small room. There lay Mr Mason, soaked in blood. I began to clean his wounds. From the next room I heard the snarling, scratching noises of a wild beast or fiend.

'She bit me,' wept Mason. 'She sucked my blood. She said she would drain my heart.'

'I warned you not to visit her alone,' frowned Mr Rochester.

Mason failed to master his tears. 'I will leave Thornfield in the morning,' he whimpered. 'Take care of her, Rochester. Treat her tenderly.'

'I have always done my best and will continue to do so.' Mr Rochester seemed impatient. Later, as he escorted me back to my room, he sighed. 'Mason has the power to deprive me of happiness for ever.'

The mystery of the third storey was not destined to occupy my thoughts for long. A letter arrived, telling me that my cousin, John Reed, was dead. Mrs Reed, in her shock, had suffered a stroke. In her delirium, she had called for me.

'Promise me that you will stay only a week,' demanded Mr Rochester.

My aunt received me coldly. 'I have called you here to ease my mind before I die,' she explained.

'I have done you a wrong. It is a mere trifle but I must relieve myself of the burden. Read this.' She handed me a letter. 'It came three years ago.'

The letter was from a man called John Eyre, in Madeira. Mrs Reed explained that he was my father's brother, my uncle. In his letter, he said that, being childless, he wished to adopt me, his niece, and bequeath me his considerable wealth.

'I told him you died at Lowood,' Mrs Reed confessed. 'I didn't want you to inherit his money.'

'Aunt, you have my full forgiveness. Ask now for god's.'

Within days, she was dead.

It was midsummer eve when I returned to Thornfield. The gentle sky promised well for the future. My heart leapt when I saw Mr Rochester alone in the garden.

'Jane!' he cried. 'How like a ghost you are, appearing from nowhere in the evening light.'

'Sir, I have been with my aunt, who is dead.'

'Ah, so you *have* come from the other world!' His smile spread sunshine over me.

'I am glad to return to you,' I admitted. 'Wherever you are is my only home.'

Mr Rochester looked thoughtful. 'Jane, before you left, I had thought to marry Miss Ingram.'

I stepped away from him. 'Then I must leave you, sir. I may be poor and plain, but I am your equal in feeling. No, I am your superior, for I would scorn such a marriage.' I could not contain my sobs. 'Oh, I wish I had never been born.'

Mr Rochester seemed agitated. 'I learned the truth of my heart during your absence, Jane. I cannot marry Miss Ingram. She has no soul, whereas you have a soul of fire. You are indeed my superior. Jane, I offer you my hand and my heart. Will you pass through life at my side? Will you be my bride?'

I stared at him.

'Are you happy, Jane?'

'I am very happy.'

'Then this will atone,' he smiled.

I experienced a period of bliss as we prepared for our wedding. I could play Mr Rochester's character excellently. Rather than submission to my future husband, I teased him and kept him cross and crusty. On the whole I think he was excellently entertained.

My only cause of unease was the difference in our wealth. I would always be dependent upon him, which troubled me. I wondered whether I should contact my uncle in Madeira. A little independence would make me happier. It was a good idea, but I didn't write.

Mr Rochester was disappointed when I showed no interest in the fine clothes and jewels he offered.

'I would rather have your confidence than your wealth,' I explained. 'There must be no secrets between us.'

'Do not long for poison, Jane,' he warned.

Perhaps human beings are not meant to enjoy complete happiness in this world.

The night before our wedding, I was woken from a restless sleep by a noise in my room. Through the darkness, I saw something standing close to where I had hung my wedding dress. The creature, tall with thick hair, put on my veil and moved towards my mirror. It was not Grace Poole. Reflected in the mirror, I saw purple, swollen lips and a dark

furrowed brow. Bloodshot eyes rolled within a savage face. I shook with fear. Was it a ghost? A vampire?

As the clock struck midnight, the being tore my veil in two and brought her candle close to my face. I must have fainted then, for I remember nothing more.

When I explained all this to Mr Rochester the next morning, he shuddered and held me close. 'I will explain it all when we have been married a year and a day,' he promised.

Our wedding was to take place in a humble church. During the ceremony, Mr Rochester looked at me with love and tenderness. My heart swelled with happiness.

The clergyman said, 'If either of you know any impediment why you may not be joined together in matrimony, confess it now,' and I noticed my groom clench his jaw. His flaming eyes betrayed his impatience.

The short silence was broken by a voice from the back of the church. 'The marriage cannot go on.'

Mr Rochester moved slightly. 'Proceed,' he urged the clergyman.

'The marriage cannot proceed,' continued the voice. 'Mr Rochester is already married, and his wife is still living.'

I looked to Mr Rochester for reassurance. His face was colourless marble. His hot hand held mine firmly.

'He is married to my sister, Bertha Mason.'

I recognised the voice. I turned to see Richard Mason walking towards us.

Mr Rochester did not deny the accusation. He was indeed married, and our wedding could not proceed. 'Return to Thornfield with me,' he grimly invited the clergyman and Richard Mason. He held me close, his dark eyes desperate to see understanding and forgiveness in mine. 'I will show you my wife.'

Once back at Thornfield, Mr Rochester led us up the stairs to the third storey. Quietly unlocking a door he smiled a joyless smile. 'Meet Mrs Rochester.'

Inside the darkened room, Grace Poole sat quietly sewing. 'Take care, sir,' she warned.

In the shadows at the far end of the room, a dark figure squatted, growling like a wild beast.

Seeing her visitors, she gave a fierce cry and rose to her feet. I recognised the swollen purple face I had seen in my mirror the night before.

'We should leave,' whispered Mason.

'Go to the devil!' growled Mr Rochester.

In one violent movement the lunatic sprang at her husband, sinking her teeth into his cheek. She displayed great strength as he struggled, with the help of Grace Poole, to tie her arms and fasten her to a chair, where she continued to shriek.

'*This* is my wife,' Mr Rochester smiled grimly to the shocked clergyman. 'This is the woman I was tricked into marrying fifteen years ago.

And *this,*' he touched my shoulder, 'this girl who stands so quietly at the mouth of hell, is the wife I wished to have.'

That afternoon, Mr Rochester explained everything to me. 'Fifteen years ago, my father tricked me into marrying beautiful, wealthy Bertha Mason of Jamaica. She dazzled me,' he admitted, 'but I knew nothing about her. Oh, I was a fool! My new wife was uncontrolled; the mad child of a lunatic mother.'

He tried to persuade me to stay, as his mistress rather than his wife. I burned inside, longing for the temporary heaven he offered, but I knew that I could not be his on those terms.

'You condemn me to a wretched life,' he cried, grabbing me violently and threatening never to let me go. Our eyes met, and he released me, weeping. 'What is the point?' he cried. 'It is you, wild, free, virtuous and pure that I want, not your brittle frame.'

'I am going, sir.'

He threw himself on the sofa. 'Oh Jane, my life, my love.'

'God bless you, my dear master.'

That night, I fled, without money or possessions. I put my trust in god.

I had nowhere and nobody to run to. I begged a lift in a coach, caring not where it was heading. It was my first experience of begging, but not my last.

I slept in woods. I ate berries, drank from streams, and fought the temptation to return to Thornfield. I sought work in the villages I passed, but found only suspicion and unfriendliness. My increasingly untidy appearance led people to shun me rather than feed me.

After days of friendless wandering I was weak and desperately hungry. I saw a house with a warm light glowing from the window.

I struggled towards it but, reaching it, dared not knock upon the door. I  sank, weeping on the doorstep. 'I can but die. I will await god's will.'

'God does not will that you die on my doorstep,' said a man's voice. He carried me inside and somebody fed me. I must have been very weak, for I could not rise from the bed in which they laid me for three days.

My host, who introduced himself as Mr St John Rivers, was a poor clergyman. He lived in Moor House with his two sisters. They offered me their hospitality for as long as I should need it. I told them my name was Jane Elliot.

'Are you married, Jane Elliot?'

I wept. They had the sensitivity to ask no further questions.

As the weeks passed I grew uncomfortable relying upon the charity of my new friends, who had little to spare. I found employment as mistress of a small charity school in the village, and moved into my own small home next to the school. I felt busy and useful. I ought to have been happy.

One day, visiting my three friends, I found them reading a letter. The ladies were tearful. 'Our Uncle John is dead,' explained St John. 'We did not know him well, but we thought perhaps he might leave us a little money. It seems that he has left everything to another, unknown relative.'

I felt their disappointment. The sisters would soon have to find work. Their cosy family home would have to be sold.

Over time, I realised that St John lacked his sisters' warmth. He used his eyes to discover other people's thoughts rather than to reveal his own. His hard character took away my liberty of mind. He gained influence over me with his cold determination. With such people I can never find a middle way between absolute submission and determined revolt. I submitted to St John.

One day, he visited me with news. 'I will soon leave to be a missionary,' he told me.

This did not surprise me. His nature was the kind of rock from which heroes, lawgivers and statesmen are hewn.

'I should like you to join me, Jane.'

This did surprise me.

'God is calling you, through me, to be his servant. Of course, we must marry first. It would be unthinkable for you to accompany me otherwise. I claim you for god's service, not for my pleasure.'

No longer able to submit to his will, I burst into volcanic revolt. 'I scorn your cold idea of marriage,' I trembled, 'and I scorn you for offering it.'

'I will wait for you to change your mind,' he frowned, standing to leave. Suddenly, he stopped.

Something on the corner of a picture I had been sketching earlier caught his eye. Moving quickly, he tore a corner from the paper and left the room.

The following morning, a very different, rather flushed St John found me. 'What is your real name?' he demanded. 'If you are Jane Eyre, then you must read this.'

I reached for the letter he held out to me. 'You had scribbled your name on the corner of your sketch. I saw it yesterday,' he explained.

The letter was from a solicitor in London. He was searching for a person called Jane Eyre, who must be found immediately, for her uncle, Mr Eyre of Madeira, had died recently, leaving her all his property.

'You are rich,' smiled St John.

If he expected me to leap for joy, he was disappointed. My uncle had been my only living relative, and now he was dead. I was not ungrateful, however. My heart swelled with the knowledge of my independent wealth.

'Perhaps you should ask how much you are worth?'

'How much?' I obeyed.

'Twenty thousand pounds.'

This took my breath. I felt like a person with a small appetite sitting at a feast for a hundred. A thought suddenly struck me. Something did not quite make sense.

'Why did this solicitor contact *you*?' I asked.

St John was reluctant to answer. 'You will find me cold on that point.'

'But I am hot, and fire melts ice,' I replied.

'Very well. Mr John Eyre was my uncle too. You are our mystery relative. We are cousins, Jane.'

Here was real wealth! Wealth to my heart!

I was filled with joy. I was no longer alone. I had family, and I could help them. 'You must all share this wealth!' I exclaimed.

'We will be your cousins anyway, you need not make this sacrifice.'

'It is no sacrifice. We can all be together and independent.'

Some months later, my three cousins and I were all settled comfortably in Moor House. St John frequently reminded me of my duty to join him in god's work. I no longer saw him as flesh, but as marble. If I married him, this good man would kill me with his coldness.

One evening, as I sat quietly with my cousins, I heard a sound which made my heart stand still. Startled, my eyes and ears waited for more. My flesh quivered. 'Oh god, what is it?' I gasped.

I heard it again. A voice somewhere cried 'Jane! Jane! Jane!' It was a voice I knew and loved.

It called wildly, eerily, in pain and grief.

'I am coming!' I cried, running into the garden. 'Wait for me. Where are you?'

The hills answered me with silence.

Filled with energy and resolve, I needed only to await daybreak.

After a journey of two days, my coach put me down near to Thornfield. Longing to see that familiar house, I walked quickly, sometimes running.

Imagine my shock when, instead of a stately house, I found a blackened ruin. Thornfield had been completely destroyed by fire. I stood and stared in horror.

I decided to walk to the village. I needed to know. Was Mr Rochester still alive? If so, where would I find him? I called at the inn, where the innkeeper agreed to answer my questions.

'Thornfield was burned down some months ago,' he recalled. 'The fire broke out at dead of night.'

I shuddered. I knew how the fire had started.

'Was Mr Rochester home?'

'Yes, unluckily for him. He helped all of his servants out of the house, then went back in. The servants say he went to rescue a mad wife he kept locked up in there. He followed her onto the roof where they heard him call, "Bertha!" The next minute, she jumped to her death on the stones below.'

'What happened to Mr Rochester?' I dreaded the answer. 'Is he alive?'

'Yes, but he would be better dead. He lost one hand and the sight of both eyes. He lives about thirty miles away, at Ferndean, a desolate spot.'

The following evening, I arrived at Ferndean. It was indeed a desolate place. Entering discreetly through a back door, I persuaded an astonished Mrs Fairfax to allow me to carry Mr Rochester's supper to him.

When I entered his room, I paused, attempting to calm my emotions. The face of the man I loved was desperate and brooding, his inner fire extinguished.

'Your supper, sir,' I said gently.

Mr Rochester lifted his face, but his blind eyes saw nothing. 'Who is there?' he gasped. 'I thought I heard Jane's voice. What sweet madness has seized me? Speak again, elf.'

'I am here, sir, and my heart is here too.'

'Let me touch you.' He groped in his personal darkness.

I put down the tray, walked to him, held him and kissed his blind, scarred eyes. 'I will never leave you again, sir. I will be your hand and eyes. I will read to you, walk with you, sit with you and wait on you.'

'But you will be revolted by my wounds.' His tears now mixed with mine. 'Jane, am I hideous to look at?'

'Yes, sir, you always were.'

'Only four days ago, Jane, I gave up all hope of seeing you again. I longed for you with all my soul. In anguish, I cried "Jane! Jane! Jane!"'

A chill ran down my spine, but I said nothing.

'And then, in the darkness, I thought I heard your voice on the wind. I thought I heard you say, 'I am coming! Wait for me!'

Reader, I married him. Ten years have now passed and we are supremely blessed. We suit each other perfectly. In my husband's presence I am thoroughly alive, and he in mine. The passage of time and the growth of happiness have helped to effect a gradual improvement in my husband's health. He recovered some of the sight in one of his eyes, sufficiently to see our first-born son.

Mr Rochester's inner fire burns again, and I am as happy as a human can be on this earth.

TAKING THINGS FURTHER

The real read

This *Real Reads* version of *Jane Eyre* is a retelling of Charlotte Brontë's magnificent work. If you would like to read the full, original novel, many complete editions are available, from bargain paperbacks to beautifully-bound hardbacks. You may well find a copy in your local library or charity shop.

Filling in the spaces

The loss of so many of Charlotte Brontë's original words is a sad but necessary part of the shortening process. We have had to make some difficult decisions, omitting subplots and details, some important, some less so, but all interesting. We may also, at times, have taken the liberty of combining two events into one, or of giving a character words or actions that originally belong to another. The points below will fill in some of the gaps, but nothing can beat the original.

- John Reed has two sisters who are also cruel to Jane. The adult John Reed dies by committing suicide.

- Bessie, Mrs Reed's servant, later becomes a friend to Jane.

- Jane's mother married a clergyman. Her family, feeling that she married beneath her, disowned her. They both died of typhus in Jane's first year. Her mother's brother, Mr Reed, promised to care for the baby.

- Most of the deaths at Lowood are caused by typhus. Helen, however, dies of tuberculosis.

- Adèle is possibly Mr Rochester's daughter from an affair he had with a French dancer called Céline.

- Mr Rochester was disinherited by his family until his brother died. His life has hardened his character. His family tricked him into marrying Bertha Mason for financial reasons.

- Bertha and Richard Mason were born in Jamaica. Bertha's mother was a Creole.

- Blanche Ingram and her mother are proud and cold.

- For his house party Mr Rochester dresses as a gypsy to trick his guests. When the 'gypsy' tells Blanche Ingram that he is not as wealthy as she thinks, she grows cold towards him.

- The wedding is stopped by Mr Briggs, a solicitor, who has been sent by John Eyre, Jane's uncle in Madeira. He was her father's brother. He learnt of the marriage from Richard Mason.

- John Eyre is also uncle to St John Rivers and his sisters.

Back in time

Charlotte Brontë was born in Yorkshire in 1816, the third of six children. She lost her mother and her two elder sisters to tuberculosis at an early age. For many years her father was the curate of the parish church at Howarth in Yorkshire, a county in the north of England. The moorland landscape around

Howarth is vividly described in *Jane Eyre*. The four surviving Brontë children played on the moors, and spent much of their rather isolated lives studying and writing. The three girls continued writing into their adult lives.

Jane Eyre, published in 1847, is Charlotte Brontë's best known work. She also wrote *Shirley* and *Villette*. Her sister Emily wrote *Wuthering Heights*, whilst the third sister, Anne, is best known for *The Tenant of Wildfell Hall*.

In writing *Jane Eyre*, Charlotte Brontë draws upon some of her own experiences, particularly when describing events at Lowood. Childhood mortality rates were high in Victorian England, although swift advances in medicine would soon improve this.

A woman's place in Victorian society was difficult. It was not easy to become established as a published writer, and the Brontë sisters all used male pseudonyms to improve the chances of their work being published. It was hard to achieve financial security if you were a woman, and for many the only options were a prudent marriage or, like Jane Eyre, work as a governess.

Victorian women were expected to be quiet, content and controlled. Although Jane Eyre behaves appropriately, she expresses her frustration with the limitations placed upon women, compared with the opportunities available to men. Although she is dutiful, she is not submissive. Bertha Mason, perhaps by deliberate contrast, is unable to control her passions. This has led many readers to wonder whether Bertha's madness is partly because her freedom to express her true nature has been limited by conventional Victorian attitudes to women.

Finding out more

We recommend the following books, websites and films to gain a greater understanding of Charlotte Brontë and the world she lived in.

Books

● Ann Dinsdale and Simon Warner, *The Brontës at Howarth*, Frances Lincoln, 2006.

- Terry Deary, *Vile Victorians* (Horrible Histories), Scholastic, 1994.

- Jean Rhys, *Wide Sargasso Sea*, Penguin Modern Classics, 2001. First published in 1966, this is a challenging read in which Jean Rhys tells the story of Antionette (Bertha) Mason before she met Rochester. Rhys blames Bertha's madness upon Rochester's rejection of her and her Creole background.

- Emily Brontë, *Wuthering Heights*, many editions available, including a *Real Reads* version.

Websites

- www.bronte.org.uk
Home of the Brontë Museum and the Brontë Society, based at the Howarth Parsonage in which the Brontës lived. The Museum is well worth a visit if you are visiting West Yorkshire.

- www.howarth-village.org.uk/brontes
Information about the Brontës and Brontë country.

- http://en.wikipedia.org/wiki/jane_eyre
Provides useful information about the text and its author.

- www.victorianweb.org
Scholarly information on all aspects of Victorian life, including literature, history and culture.

- www.bbc.co.uk/history/british/victorians
The BBC's interactive site about Victorian Britain, with a wide range of information and activities for all ages.

Films

- *Jane Eyre*, BBC, 1983. Directed by Julian Amyes.

- *Jane Eyre*, Miramax, 1996. Directed by Franco Zeffirelli.

- *Jane Eyre*, BBC, 2007.

Food for thought

Here are some things to think about if you are reading *Jane Eyre* alone, or ideas for discussion if you are reading it with friends.

In retelling *Jane Eyre* we have tried to recreate, as accurately as possible, Charlotte Brontë's original plot and characters. We have also tried to imitate aspects of her style. Remember, however, that this is not the original work; thinking about the points below, therefore, can only help you begin to understand Charlotte Brontë's craft. To move forward from here, turn to the full-length version of *Jane Eyre* and lose yourself in her wonderful writing.

Starting points

- Which characteristics in Jane's personality remain unchanged throughout the story? How does she change?

- What do you think are the main differences between Jane and Helen Burns?

- When do you feel most sympathy for Jane? Why? When do you most admire her? Why?

- How do you feel about Mr Rochester? Do your feelings change?

- Compare Mr Rochester with St John Rivers. Which of them do you prefer? Why?

- What do you think about Mr Rochester's treatment of Bertha Mason?

- Was Jane right to marry Mr Rochester at the end of the story?

Themes

What do you think Charlotte Brontë is saying about the following themes in *Jane Eyre*?

- passion and restraint

- adventure

- women's lives

- wealth and social class

Style

Can you find paragraphs containing examples of the following?

- descriptions of scenery and weather

- the use of short sentences to create suspense

- imagery of fire and ice

Look closely at how these paragraphs are written. What do you notice? Can you write a paragraph in the same style?

Symbols

We see many symbols in everyday life. Writers frequently use symbols in their work to help the reader's understanding. Consider how the symbols below match the action.

- fire
- heat and cold
- eyes
- stone